SUMMERHOUSE TIME

Eileen Spinelli

SUMMERHOUSE TIME

Illustrated by Joanne Lew-Vriethoff

Alfred A. Knopf 🐎 New York

THIS IS A BORZOI BOOK PUBLISHED BY ALFRED A. KNOPF

Published in the United States by Alfred A. Knopf, an imprint of
Random House Children's Books, a division of Random House, Inc., New York.

KNOPF, BORZOI BOOKS, and the colophon are registered trademarks of
Random House, Inc.

www.randomhouse.com/kids

Educators and librarians, for a variety of teaching tools, visit us at
www.randomhouse.com/teachers

Library of Congress Cataloging-in-Publication Data
Spinelli, Eileen.
Summerhouse time / by Eileen Spinelli ; illustrations by Joanne Lew-Vriethoff.
— 1st ed.
p. cm.
SUMMARY: The approach of summerhouse time at the beach brings new
experiences and good memories of this annual tradition, of aunts, uncles,
cousins, and grandparents laughing, eating, playing, and relaxing.
ISBN: 978-0-375-84061-6 (trade)
ISBN: 978-0-375-94061-3 (lib. bdg.)
[1. Summer—Fiction. 2. Beaches—Fiction. 3. Family life—Fiction.]
I. Lew-Vriethoff, Joanne, ill. II. Title.
PZ7.S7566Su 2007
[E]—dc22
2006024254

Printed in the United States of America

May 2007

10 9 8 7 6 5 4 3 2 1

First Edition

With thanks to my husband and dearest friend, Jerry Spinelli,
who is a steadfast and loving support
in my writing and in my life.

Thank you as well to our son Kevin James
for his brave personal insights.

To Jean Galleone, who knows opera.

To Ellyn Martin and Linda Voelker,
who answered my questions about cats and Seattle.

Thank you to my inspiring editor, Cecile Goyette,
who went beyond the call of duty on this project.

And as ever—to our children, their spouses, and our grandchildren,
whose beautiful and much-loved spirits peek through
the pages of this and all my books.

First Saturday in June

Fifty-nine days to go.

I can't find my purple beach towel.
I can't even get to my closet
without walking across
a sea of dirty socks.

Mom pokes her head into my doorway,
says:
"Time to clean your room, Sophie."
And I have to admit
she's right.

And it's not that cleaning my room
is the worst thing to do.
It's just that there are so many other
better things to do,
like—
painting my toenails Strawberry Pink,
eating a huge stack of Uncle Joe's pancakes,
dreaming of riding the Ferris wheel,
thinking up a story to tell
around the campfire
on Scary Story Night,

painting shells,
riding waves . . .
all the fun, wonderful,
sandy, sunny things we do
at Summerhouse Time.

New Boy

There's a new kid
on our block.
A boy.
Usually I don't
pay much attention
to boys.
But there's something
about this boy—
his loud laugh
when his beagle puppy
jumps on him,
his T-shirt that says
WONDERKID,
his shy smile that says

he doesn't really
believe it.

Mom

Mom is a substitute teacher.
She never works more than
three days a week.
She could work summers at the Y
to earn extra money.
But Mom's favorite saying is:
"The best things in life
aren't things."
I know we have
just one credit card
(for emergencies only).
I know we have
the smallest house
of all my relatives.
Mom grins, says:
"Fewer windows to wash!"
And the oldest car.
"Owned free and clear!"
Mom beams.

When I asked
for a PlayStation
a couple of years ago,
Mom tweaked my cheek, said:
"Sophie, dear,
the whole *world*
is your play station!"

Well, *maybe*.

Dad's Part-Time Job

Today Dad is driving
the mulch truck
for Liggett's Landscaping.
He's been doing odd jobs
for Mr. Liggett
every summer
forever.

But *never* in August.

"August is only
Summerhouse Time,"
says Dad.

And that's how it's been
forever.

DAD'S FULL-TIME JOB

Dad teaches American history
at Hamilton High School.
And when he's not teaching
American history,
he's reading
or watching something about
or talking about . . .
American history!
At the dinner table.
In the car.
While we play Monopoly.
He's even been known to
poke his head out from the shower
to tell us something like:

Abraham Lincoln
kept his important papers
in his hat!

When President Andrew Jackson died,
his parrot had to be "escorted"
from the funeral because
it was swearing.

George Washington made sure
his horse's teeth
were brushed every day.

Theodore Roosevelt's kids
used to sled down the White House stairs
on cookie trays.

John Quincy Adams liked to swim
in the Potomac River
naked!

Thanks, Dad!

SUMMER SUPPLIES

It's so hot.
So hot.
So Mom and I walk
to the Book Bin.

The Book Bin sells
used books, magazines, board games,
posters, and puzzles.

And the Book Bin
is air-conditioned!

We buy a Scrabble game
(only one *E* missing),
a fifty-cent bag
of paperback mysteries
for Grandmom,
a 1,000-piece puzzle
of the Lincoln Memorial
for Dad.
I have never seen
my father put together *any* puzzle.
Mom shrugs.

"If we get enough rainy days,
he might."

Mom gets herself another
thick book on "simple living."
"Don't we already live
simple enough?"
I ask.
(I'm thinking about our
no-air-conditioning house.)

I get another
copy of *Anne of Green Gables*.
"Don't you already have that?"
Mom asks.
(Actually, this one makes three.)
On Thanksgiving,
my baby cousin James
spit up on my favorite copy.
It still stinks!

Suddenly Mom spies it:
a "teach yourself Italian" kit for kids.
"Sophie, look—

you can teach yourself
itali-ano!"

"But, Mom,
the beach is in
New Jersey."

We gather all these
bits and things
for Summerhouse Time.

TWITCH

New Boy
is walking his waggly puppy.
I see him
from my window.
My heart is twitching.
(I think it is.)
I sort of giggle,
want to tell someone
what I'm
sort of feeling.

Dad is out driving
the mulch truck.
Mom is out weeding
the garden.
Besides,
I'm not so sure
they are ready for this.
I turn to Orange the cat,
who is curled up
on my bed.
I say it to her:
"Orange,
I think I'm in love—
sort of."

Invitation

My cousin Tammy phones.
"Hi, Soapy!"
Tammy is five
and calls me Soapy
because when she was
really little
she couldn't say Sophie.

"Hi, Tammy."
"Soapy, you're invited to
my birthday party
on July the second."
I act surprised—
even though I've known about it
for a week.
"Soapy, don't forget to bring
a present."
"I won't."
"Soapy, Daddy ordered me
a mermaid cake!"
"Wow!"
"A chocolate mermaid cake!"
"Double wow."

"Soapy, do you want to say hello
to Baby James?"
(I can hear Baby James
howling in the background.)
"Not today," I tell her.
"Soapy, can I say hello to Orange?"
"Orange is taking a nap, Tammy."
"Well, tell her she's invited, too."
"I will."
"And, Soapy?"
"Yes, Tammy?"
"Tell her don't forget
to bring a present."
"Okay, Tammy."

Brainstorming

I'm trying to think of ways
to actually meet
New Boy.
Like maybe:

Bake dog biscuits
for his beagle.

(I found a recipe
in one of Mom's
"simple living" books.)

Or:

Write my name and address
on the bottom of
one of my flip-flops
and "lose" it
on his lawn.

Or:

"Return" his puppy's chew toy.
(I would buy one at the dollar store.)
He'll say: "That's not my puppy's chew toy."
I'll say: "Oh, I thought it was."

Or:

Pretend to pass out
from the heat
on Wonderkid's driveway.
So he can save me.

MISSING

I miss Katie Johnson,
my best friend.
She lives with her mom,
but every summer
she goes away to stay with her dad
in Seattle.
I haven't seen her
since school let out.
We've e-mailed
back and forth a little.
But that gets tricky.
Mom and Dad and I
share one computer.
I don't get much time on it.
Besides—life in Seattle
sounds pretty exciting.
Katie is having lunch
in the Space Needle.
She's going crabbing
on Puget Sound.
She sent me a picture of herself and her dad
with a big fish in their arms
at Pike Place Market.

(I always send her a postcard
once we get to the beach.)
After a few weeks,
our e-mails stop.

Today I hear New Boy
laughing outside with his puppy.
I don't think he's missing anyone.

Thirty-four days to go.

Uh-oh

Dad comes home
from hauling mulch,
hot,
tired,
cranky.

He shoos Orange
off the chair.

He tells Mom
he's not hungry.

He growls about
my flip-flops
being under the table.

He talks back
to the TV.
He falls asleep
sitting up.

Later
he apologizes,
takes us out
for ice cream cones.
Mom gets cherry vanilla,
I get chocolate almond.
Dad gets strawberry
but eats only half.

Something's still wrong.

Last year,
Tammy's birthday party
was at the Biglerville Zoo.
Aunt Liz is
the zoo's special-events director.

That means
our whole family
gets in free.

It means
we get to meet people like
Primate Pete,
Tarzana the Storyteller,
Bertha the Bird Lady.

Once, Tammy and I
even got to watch
Dr. Weber, the vet,
extract a tooth
from an alligator
named Arnold.

Last year,
when Tammy's other
grandmother was standing
in front of the lion's cage
eating her ice cream and cake,
the lion peed on her!

So this year
the party is
at Tammy's house.

Thirty days to go.

Grandparents

Tammy calls her other grandmother
Mom-mom
and her other grandfather
Pop-pop.

It must be nice
to have two whole sets
of grandparents.

I have only one set.
Dad's parents died
when he was fifteen.

Dad says
they would have loved me
to pieces.

Tammy's Birthday Party

Tammy's birthday party
feels like
a mini summerhouse preview.
There's Tammy's parents:
Aunt Liz and Uncle Dave.
And little brother Baby James
howling for a balloon.
There's Grandmom and Grandpop.
Mom and Dad and me.
(But not Orange—who sent
regrets *and* a present.)

Aunt Nancy and Uncle Joe
and my cousins Colleen and Cooper
live too far away
to make it to the party.
But Aunt Nancy calls,
and she and Uncle Joe
sing "Happy Birthday" to Tammy
over the phone
really loud!
Tammy is already wearing their gift—
a mermaid bathing suit and goggles.

I say a quick hello
to my cousin Colleen.
"Are you getting excited
about Summerhouse Time?"
I ask.
"I guess so,"
says Colleen.
She guesses so?

Every year
on Tammy's birthday,
Dad makes
this comment:
"You know, folks,
Tammy's birthday
is when the Continental Congress
really declared independence.
It was July the *second*,
not the fourth!"

And then he whips out
a sparkler and lights it
along with the candles
on Tammy's cake.

This year,
Dad makes no comment,
lights no sparkler.

The others
don't seem to notice.
But I do.

I notice when Dad goes off by himself
to the back corner of the yard
while the rest of us sing
"Happy Birthday."
What's going on?

FINALLY

I met him!
I met him!
I met him!

New Boy, New Boy, New Boy!

I didn't bake dog biscuits
or lose my flip-flop
or return a chew toy
or faint in his driveway
(I could've clonked my head).

I simply climbed
halfway up the maple tree
in his side yard
and waited.

When he came outside
I hollered, "Help!"
and pretended to be afraid
to climb down.
And true to the name
on his T-shirt,
he climbed up after me.

First Conversation

"What were you doing
up in the tree?"
"I was looking for my cat."
(Is my nose growing?
Am I getting really red?)

I knew very well
where Orange was—
under our porch, keeping cool.
Sensible cat.

"Is your cat lost?"
"I wouldn't say lost,
exactly.
Orange knows her way home."
"I have a dog."
"I know, a beagle.
It's cute."
"It's a she, Dakota."
"My name is Sophie.
Sophie Bolton.
I live right across the street."
"I'm Jimmy Gabbiano.
Nice to meet you."
"Gabbiano . . .
Isn't that Italian?"

BEST MOM

Later that day
I ask Mom:
"Do you think
they still have
that Italian kit for kids
at the Book Bin?"

Mom shakes her head.
"Nope, it's gone."

"Rats!"

"I bought it."

"You did?"

"Uh-huh.
I thought I'd bring it
to the summerhouse.
Just in case."

I throw my arms
around my mother,
nearly knock her over.
"Did anyone ever tell you
you're the best mom
in the whole world?"

"You're the first one today."

First Lesson

The Italian kit contains:
A book of words with pictures.
A CD.
A map of Italy.
A small Italian flag.
I tape the map of Italy
to my wall.
I put the flag in my pencil can.
I open the book.
The first page says:
"*La casa*—house."
Then words I already know:
la radio,
il poster,
il compact disc.
I write words I don't know
on Post-its and stick them
everywhere.

La lampada on my lamp,
il cassettone on my bureau.
In my bathroom it's
il bagno.
I stick a Post-it on
la vasca (the tub).

On the toilet—*il water*
(*il water*, really??).
On the sink—*il lavandino*.
"Toilet paper" is
la carta igienica.
Yikes!
How do you pronounce
i-g-i-e-n-i-c-a?
I guess *il compact disc*
will tell me.

I will listen later.
For now I skim ahead
in the book
to look for words like
boy . . .
girl . . .
love.

SECOND LESSON

"Boy" is *ragazzo*.
"Girl" is *ragazza*.

But I can't find
the word for *love*
at first.
And then I giggle,
because I already know
the word.
I've heard Grandpop
sing it a hundred times—
that funny song
about moons
and big pizza pies
hitting you in the eye—
"that's *amore*."
The word for "love"
in Italian is
a-mo-re.
As in
Sophie Bolton *amores*
Jimmy Gabbiano.

Molto Italiano

I'm going crazy, *matto*, with Italian.
I mean *italiano*.

Spaghetti!
Pizza!
Uno!
Due!
Tre!
Quattro!
Gatto!
(Means "cat," not "five.")

"What's all this about?"
says Dad.

"*Amore,*"
says Mom.

I'm too shocked
to deny it.
Mom *knows*.
"Love?" says Dad.
"She's only eleven."

Mom kisses the top
of Dad's head.
"Now, Mike,
you haven't forgotten

old Ginger Davies already,
have you?"

"Ginger was twelve."

"Yes, but *you*
were *eleven*."

Dad covers his ears.

"Orecchie," I say.

Dad looks at me.
"Huh?"

"Orecchie," I say.
"Ears."

CIAO

I'm not stupid.
I know that Jimmy Gabbiano
wasn't born in Italy.
But *somebody* in his family was.

Maybe even his parents
(I haven't met them yet).
Or his grandparents.
Someone. Sometime.

The next time I see Jimmy Gabbiano,
I waltz right on over.
I say, *"Ciao"*—
sounds like "chow," means "hi"—
"amico"—
means "friend."

"Huh?" says Jimmy.
I repeat:
"Ciao, amico."

He frowns.
"What's that, Spanish?"
Mamma mia!
(Means "oh boy!")

PRACTICE

I practice my Italian
on Orange.

She's sitting on my windowsill,
looking out.

I tell her:
"You are *il gatto*,
a cat.
Dakota is *la cane*,
a dog.
You are looking out
la finestra,
the window.
Soon we will be going to
the *estate-casa*,
the summerhouse."

Orange jumps down
from the windowsill
and wanders out *la porta*.

I call after her:
"I'm going to look up
the Italian word
for 'sourpuss.' "

Riding Bikes

Jimmy and I
ride our bikes
to the little park
near the library.
It has stopped raining,
but the benches
are still wet,
so we go sit
under the band-shell roof.

"How's the Italian coming?"
he asks.
"Good," I say. *"Bene."*

"What made you want
to take up Italian?"

"Oh, it was just my mom's idea.

"It's almost Summerhouse Time,"
I tell him.

"What's that?"

"Just my favorite time
of the whole year."

"Better than Christmas?"

"*Molto* better—a month at the beach.
Our rented pink cottage.
My grandmom and grandpop.
Our whole noisy family."

"Sounds cool," says Jimmy.

"It is.
You should see Dad and my uncles
dragging all the big, fat suitcases
from the cars."

"I guess you need a lot of stuff
for a whole month."

"Yep. And we have to clean the place
before we even unpack.
My grandparents give
all us kids
the cleaning stuff
and put us to work.

They call us
the Mop and Bucket Brigade.
Grandmom chases all the spiders away
with the broom."

"Spiders?"

"Yep. My aunt Nancy
is terrified of spiders."

"But spiders eat the bad bugs."

"Tell that to Aunt Nancy."

"When do you leave?"

"August first."

"That's only
four days from now."

"I know."
(He said *only*!)

We sit for a while,
raindrops dripping,
late July air steamy,
not talking.

Jimmy must be thinking about
what I just told him—
how in four days I'll be gone
for *a whole month*.

He's probably missing me already.
Maybe even thinking about
kissing me?!
It will be
my first kiss.
Il primo bacio.
I start to get goose bumps.

Jimmy turns to me.
"I was just thinking . . . ,"
he says.
"What about?"

"I was thinking
that spiders don't really
eat their victims."

"What?"

"They dissolve them first.
They drink them."

"That's what you were thinking?"

"Yep."

TWO MORE DAYS

Mom gets ready to latch my big suitcase.
"Anything else you want to add?" she says.

"How about Jimmy Gabbiano?"

Mom gives me a look.

"I'm serious."
"So am I."

"Sometimes when you're in the middle of
a red-hot love affair, it's a good idea
to cool off for a while."

"I think he's already cooled.
I think he's more interested in spiders than me."

"Oh well, then," says Mom,
"this is the best thing that can happen."
"Huh?"
"Sure. You're going away for a month.
That gives him a whole month
to miss you.
I bet he won't be
so cool
when you come back."

I hadn't thought of that.
Is Mom right?
I picture Jimmy Gabbiano running toward me
a month from now,
saying he missed me.

Cool!

On the Porch

Jimmy and I
are sitting on my porch.
The moon is bright yellow.
Orange is chasing fireflies.
It's *sooo* hot.

I'm rubbing an ice cube
up and down my arm.
Jimmy is eating a Popsicle.
I say: "Do you want
to write to each other?"
"Write?"
"Yeah. While I'm gone."
"Do you mean e-mail?"
"No. We don't take our computer.
I mean write-write. Notes and stuff."
"I'm not much of a writer."
"How about postcards?"
"I guess so."
"You can tell me
what you're doing."
"I can tell you that right now—
I'll be riding my bike,

playing with Dakota,
getting ready for school."
I feel like punching him
in the nose.
I punch his arm instead.
Not *too* hard.
He grins. "I'm kidding. Yeah—
I'll write to you."

Okay then.

DISASTER

On the last day
before we leave
Mom comes screaming
into the kitchen:
"My bathing suit doesn't fit!"
Dad looks up from his coffee.
"Did it shrink?"
"Not funny!"
Mom slumps.
"Now I have to run out
and find a new one."
Dad winks at me.
"That could take weeks."

Mom swats him with the dish towel.
But Dad is right.
The last time
Mom went looking for a bathing suit—
four years ago—
it *did* take weeks.
"Want me to come along?" I ask.
"No," says Mom. "You stay here.
Help Dad with the garden.
I'll be back
as soon as possible."

"Weeks," Dad says.
I nod.
"Weeks."

Too Much Sun

Dad's plan is to pick
all the vegetables that are ready
and take them to the summerhouse
to be in salads,
and grilled
and marinated
and pickled.

He's arranged for the Gabbianos
to pick whatever they want
while we're away.

Mr. Liggett will send someone
to weed and water.

Dad tells me to get the big basket.

When I come back from the garage
he is slouched against the fence,
white as a sheet.

I kneel down in front of him.
"Dad! What's wrong?
Should I call 911?"

Dad takes a deep breath.
"No, honey.
Just bring me a glass of water."

He drinks the water. Pats my head.
"A little too much sun. I'm fine now.

Don't tell Mom. No need to worry her.
My fault for not wearing a hat."

I want to believe he is fine.

I wish I could forget
how he looked against the fence.
I wish I could forget
when he didn't finish his ice cream cone.
I wish I could forget
how he was off by himself at Tammy's party.

I really want to believe.

SURPRISE

It's late
when Mom gets home.
She flops
into a chair,
kicks off her shoes,
and asks,
"How do you say
'I'll never shop again
as long as I live'
in Italian?"
I point to the bag
in her hand.
"Looks like you
found a bathing suit."
"No—I found this bag
on the porch.
It's for you."

I peek into the bag.

There's a box
tied with . . .
a shoelace?

I open it.
Inside I find
a necklace.
I hold it up.
On the end of the chain,
dangling like a tiny star,
is a silver spider.
There's a note in the bag.
It says:
Just in case
I'm not up
when you leave tomorrow—
have a great time.
Your friend (amico),
Jimmy
P.S. The word for "spider"
in Italian is ragno.

Uau!
(means "Wow!")

Bedtime, the Night Before

"Big day tomorrow,"
says Dad.
"Better get some sleep."

Mom sighs.
"Maybe I can borrow
a suit from Nancy.
She usually brings two."

"Maybe you can buy one
at the beach," says Dad.

Mom rolls her eyes.
"The suits at the beach
are all size zero!"

Dad points to me.
"Sleep."

I feel the silvery
spider necklace
dangling from my neck.
I sail up the stairs.

I sing out:
"*Buonanotte,
mia famiglia!*"

The First Day of August

This morning,
Orange is napping
in the cool shade
under the porch.

This morning,
Dad is stuffing
one last bag
into the car's trunk.

This morning,
I am tossing
a few more things
into my backpack:
sunblock, hair clips, books.
Then I run outside,
shine the beam
of my flashlight
under the porch.

"C'mon, Orangey cat,"
I tell her.
"It's Summerhouse Time!"

Arrivederci

Jimmy Gabbiano
is nowhere in sight.
I look up at
his bedroom window.
I waggle a finger.

"*Arrivederci, amore,*"
I whisper.

Dad's Green Chevy

It's a long, bumpy ride
to the summerhouse.
Our car sounds like this:
clinkety-clunk
clinkety-clunk
clinkety-clinkety-clunk.
Mom says:
"Hey, it gets us
where we need to go."
Dad reminds her with a grin,
"Not always."

Excited

Orange likes
riding in the car.
She falls asleep
on my lap.

I'm too excited
for sleep.
Can't wait
to rent bikes,
to fly kites,
to tell scary stories
around a sparking
driftwood fire.
But mostly,
I can't wait
to see Colleen
and show her my spider necklace
and tell her about Jimmy Gabbiano.
Colleen won't say:
"You're only eleven."
Colleen will understand.

COOL COLLEEN

Colleen is fourteen
and really cool.
She has this tiny tattoo
of a heart
on her shoulder.

It's only temporary—
but she owns a boxful
of temporary hearts,
so they seem permanent.

She also has
this great charm bracelet.
She got it
for her twelfth birthday.
My favorite charm
is the diamondy flip-flop.
Last year Colleen let me
wear her bracelet twice.
That's how nice she is.
I can't imagine
letting Tammy wear
my spider necklace.
It's not that I'm not
nice, too.
It's that Tammy
cannot be trusted.

Arrival!

We're here!
I see it!
Our summerhouse!
Mom was right—
this old car
does get us
where we need to go.
Orange is asleep.
I shake her paw.
"Orange, wake up!
We're here!"
Orange opens just one eye.
She never gets
as excited
as I do.

My Relatives

Other cars are pulling up.
Everyone is here!

Grandmom and Grandpop,
Aunt Liz and Uncle Dave,
Tammy and Baby James
(who is already howling),
Aunt Nancy and Uncle Joe,
Cooper (Colleen's brother),
who is twelve,
and . . .
Colleen! Colleen! Colleen!

WHICH ROOM?

Colleen steps out of their car.
I race over,
throw my arms around her.
"I'm so happy to see you!
I missed you so much!
I have so much to tell you.
Want to share the same room
we shared last year?
The one with the beachy wallpaper?"

"Jeez, will you calm down?
And watch the toes, please.
You're ruining my pedicure."

"Oh, sorry—
but we want
that same room,
right?
I'll tell Dad to put my stuff
in there?"

Colleen looks me in the eye.
"I asked for
a room by myself this year.
Mom said I could."

"By yourself?"

"That's what I said."

I start to ask why,
but she's already
turned away.

I stand there
in the sandy driveway,
gawking after Colleen.
If my heart were an egg,
it would be cracking.

In two seconds,
I will be bursting
into tears.

What did I do?

Then Tammy races over.
"Soapy! Soapy!
Look what I found!"

She dangles an old crab shell
in front of my nose
as I just
stand there.

Nothing

Aunt Nancy pulls me aside
into the laundry room.
"Honey, I'm really sorry
about Colleen."

"Is she mad at me?" I ask.

"She's mad at the world."

"How come?"

"I don't know.
Uncle Joe and I keep asking
what's wrong.
And she keeps saying,
'Nothing.'"

Tammy pops in, dragging
her Fuzzy Alligator.
"How can someone
keep saying nothing?"

Actually,
that's a good question.

GETTING SETTLED

It takes a while
for us to get settled.

Suitcases pop open,
spilling stuff down the stairs.

Dad and the uncles
install hook-and-eye locks
on the bathroom doors.
(Last summer,
Cooper accidentally
walked in on Grandmom!)

Mom and the aunts
go to the fish market for clams.

Grandpop
attaches a coat-hanger antenna
to the old TV.

Tammy
squiggles into
her mermaid suit.
Cooper
hunts for Orange.
Colleen
won't come out of her room.
"I'm bored already," she grumps,
loud enough for everyone to hear,
especially me.

Solo Orange

For the first few days,
Orange always has to stay
in the tiny back room.
She doesn't like it much.
But she needs time
to get used to the summerhouse,
time till it feels like home to her
once again.

First Night

By dark,
we are all put away
and clam-chowdered
and sitting on the deck.

By dark,
Baby James and Orange
have stopped howling.
They are both asleep.

By dark,
the ocean is
all silvery with stars.
And the cool beachy air
is salty-sweet.

In the dark,
Dad says:
"C'mon, Jess."
He takes Mom's hand,
leads her across the beach,
where they dance
in the thumping,

gushing,
moon-foaming surf.
Just like always.

ROOMING WITH TAMMY

Tammy says:
"I'm glad you're sleeping
in my room, Soapy."

Tammy says:
"Soapy, guess what?
I'm never *ever*
taking off
my mermaid swimsuit.
Ever!
Not for the whole month!"

Tammy says:
"Soapy, you can hold Fuzzy Alligator
if you are scared of the dark."

Tammy says:
"Soapy, want to go collecting shells
tomorrow?"

I say:
"Tammy, I'm tired now.
I want to go to sleep.
No more talking."

Tammy says:
"Okay, Soapy,
I'll just whisper."

"Whispering is still talking,"
I tell her.

Tammy says:
"Don't be all crabby
like poopy Colleen."

I say:
"Good night, Tammy!"

STUDENT

Tammy scampers
into the living room.
"Soapy, teach me how
to talk Italian."
"Be quiet," I tell her.
"I'm trying to listen to the CD.
I'm trying to hear
how to pronounce stuff."
Tammy plops onto my lap.
"I want to try, too."

After about sixty seconds
Tammy hops off my lap,
races around the summerhouse
yelling:
"*La bar-ca! La bar-ca!*
The boat! The boat!
I can talk I-tal-ian!"

BREAKFAST AT THE SUMMERHOUSE: ONE

Uncle Joe is the main cook
during Summerhouse Time.

This morning, he's wearing
Grandmom's flower-print apron
and flipping pancakes
shaped like starfish.
"Somebody get the camera!"
calls Aunt Liz.
"Somebody give me a break,"
growls growly Colleen.

Breakfast at the Summerhouse: Two

Baby James is in his high chair,
eating his oatmeal
all
by
himself.
He giggles.
He waggles his spoon.
He flicks—*splat!*
A gob of oatmeal
lands on Colleen's head.
Uh-oh.
Baby James giggles some more.
I open my mouth to laugh,
but Colleen is not laughing.

So I don't, either.
Last year,
we both would have.

Breakfast at the Summerhouse: Three

Tammy:
"Uncle Joe, will your feelings be hurt
if I don't eat your pancakes?"

Uncle Joe:
"I thought you liked my pancakes."

Tammy:
"I do like your pancakes. But
I like saltwater taffies better."

Aunt Liz:
"Sorry, Tammy. No saltwater taffies
for breakfast."

Tammy:
"Please, Mommy.
Please! Please! Please!"

Aunt Liz rolls her eyes.
Tammy turns to Uncle Dave.
"Please, Daddy.
Please! Please! Please!"

Uncle Dave hates to say no to Tammy:
"I have an idea.
How about one pancake
and one saltwater taffy?"

Tammy grins.
"Deal!"

I have my own box of saltwater taffies.
I look over at Mom.
She looks back,
says:
"Don't even
think about it."

Saltwater Taffy Fallout

Aunt Liz and Uncle Dave
aren't speaking.

Aunt Liz says
Uncle Dave is too easy on Tammy.
Uncle Dave says
Aunt Liz is too hard.

Aunt Nancy says
Aunt Liz should be glad that
Uncle Dave was so willing to
quit his job in insurance
so he could take care of
their kids while Aunt Liz
works at the job she loves
at the Biglerville Zoo.

Uncle Joe says
Aunt Nancy should mind
her own business.

Dad says
it's silly to fight
over saltwater taffies.

Mom says
we should all watch Tammy and Baby James
some night soon
so Aunt Liz and Uncle Dave
can take a long, romantic
walk in the moonlight.

Grandpop says
it's hard for a couple to be romantic
when they aren't speaking.

I hate it when
people aren't speaking.

I especially hate it
when somebody doesn't speak
to me.
I almost wish they would
holler at me.

Speaking is better
than not speaking.
That's what I say.

Grandmom says:
"Everybody to the beach!"

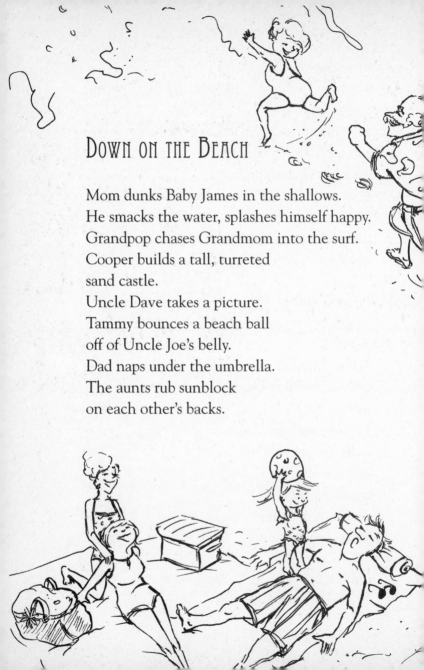

DOWN ON THE BEACH

Mom dunks Baby James in the shallows.
He smacks the water, splashes himself happy.
Grandpop chases Grandmom into the surf.
Cooper builds a tall, turreted
sand castle.
Uncle Dave takes a picture.
Tammy bounces a beach ball
off of Uncle Joe's belly.
Dad naps under the umbrella.
The aunts rub sunblock
on each other's backs.

Colleen has her nose in a book.
When I ask her what she's reading,
she doesn't answer.
I tell myself:
That's just Colleen.
Every summer
she likes to be
all wrapped up in a book.
This is just like always.

But I don't
believe myself.

NOTE

When Colleen
goes off into the water,
I ask Aunt Liz
for a notepad and pen.

I write:
Dear Colleen,
I miss hanging out together.
I miss sharing secrets.

And I've been wanting to tell you this
since we got here—
I think I'm in love.

Your best cousin,
xox, Sophie

P.S. It's not really a secret.
Mom and Dad already know.

I stick the note
in Colleen's book,
right behind her bookmark.
And I wait.

THAL-ASS-O-PHOBIA

Cooper is afraid of some water.
Not bathwater.
Not pool water.
Not pond water.
Cooper is afraid of
ocean water.
He won't even wade in

up to his ankles.
I play aqua-therapist.
I ask him:
"Are you scared of being
knocked over by a wave?"
"No."
"Scared you'll step on
a jellyfish?"

Tammy pipes up:
"I'm scared a giant shark
is going to eat me."
"Be quiet, Tammy.
It's Cooper's turn to talk."
"No," says Cooper.
"I'm not afraid
of sharks or jellyfish."

As I run out of questions
Cooper picks up a shell
in a tangle of seaweed.
"I've got thal-ass-o-phobia,"
he says.

Tammy goes bug-eyed.
"Oh, Cooper!

Are you
going to die?"

"No. It just means
fear of the sea."

"It also means," I say,
"that Cooper doesn't
have as much fun at the beach
as we do."

Tammy pats Cooper's hand.
"Poor Cooper."

I point to my cousin.
"No more poor Cooper!

Before this summer is over,
you are going to stand
in the ocean waves
at the beach."

"Oh, no," he says.
"Oh, yes!" I say.

BEING SCARED

Cooper loves it
when people are afraid
of something—
but only because
he's obsessive
about phobias.

"I'm scared of falling
into the toilet,"
says Tammy.
Cooper thinks for a moment.
He shoots me a wink.
"Flushaphobia."

"Wow!" says Tammy.
"I'm also afraid of . . .

of . . . stepping in doo-doo!"
"Poopaphobia."

"I'm afraid of bowling balls
falling on my toe," I say.
"It happened to me once."

Tammy beats Cooper to the punch:
"Ouchaphobia!"

REPLY

After my shower
and before dinner,
I see a note
taped to my door—
up high
(so Tammy can't
get to it, I bet).

The note says:
In love?
Is this a joke?
You're only eleven.

It's not signed,
but I know Colleen's handwriting
by heart.

After Dinner

It rains after dinner.
The aunts turn the kitchen
into a beauty shop.
They do each other's hair.
Mom paints Tammy's toenails
Strawberry Pink.
Dad and Uncle Joe play Scrabble with Cooper.
Cooper wins!
Uncle Dave has gone for a walk.
Alone. No umbrella.
Grandmom reads a mystery.
Grandpop puts pots under leaks,
mops up puddles,
sings from the opera *Aida:*
"Ce-les-te A-i-da,
for-ma di-vi-na . . ."

Baby James clatters spoons.
Orange tries to wriggle
off my lap.
Colleen sits by the window,
chin in her hands,
looking out.
I almost feel sorry for her.
Almost.

Talking Again

By the time Uncle Dave
comes back from his walk,
he's soaked.
Aunt Liz runs over to him,
wraps an old blanket
around his shoulders.
She says:
"Dave! Now don't you go and
get pneumonia.
We all need you.
After all,
who but you
would rub my feet
or scratch my back?"

Kainotophobia
(Fear of Change)

I definitely have
kainotophobia
because I'm hating this change
between Colleen and me.

Last year,
she gave me three
of her temporary heart tattoos.
She took me on the Ferris wheel,
curled my hair,
bought me boardwalk fudge,
showed me how to ride the waves.

Last year, we shared
the beachy-wallpaper room.
We told each other stories
and kept each other's secrets.
We promised
with our pinky fingers
to be best cousins
forever.

Last year.

This year,
Colleen stays in her room
a lot,
says no to almost
everything I say.
"Wanna look at my Italian book?"
"No."
"Want me to tell you a new secret?"
"Nuh-uh."
"Wanna play Scrabble?"
"Nope."

This year,
she says,
"I hate the stupid Ferris wheel."

This year,
she flounces off
to the beach by herself—
and rides the waves
alone.

This year,
she hardly seems to know
I'm here.
I'm supposed to be her favorite cousin.
And she hasn't even said my name
once.

This year.

First Letter

Dear Jimmy,
I skipped ahead
in my Italian book
to the page about the beach,
and guess what I found out.

A gabbiano *is a seagull!*
You are Jimmy Seagull.

I wish you had wings,
so you could fly here for a visit.

My cousin Colleen,
who used to be so nice,
is acting so weird.
I miss the old Colleen.

Okay, and you.
Just a little.

Ciao.

Your amica,
Sophie

STILL RAINING

Mom and the aunts decide
to make cinnamon rolls
for tomorrow's breakfast.

I'm going to help.
Uncle Joe says:
"Hey, you gals
are stealing my job!"
Uncle Dave takes Baby James
up to bed.
We hear him singing
off-key lullabies.
We hear Baby James
howling back at Uncle Dave.
Grandpop has nodded off
in front of the TV.
Cooper and Tammy
paint clamshells.
"Mine is going to be
a food dish
for Fuzzy Alligator,"
says Tammy.
Grandmom is over
by the window
talking to Colleen,
stroking Colleen's hair.
Colleen . . . smiles?
Colleen smiles!
Hooray!

Conversation

ONE

The kitchen smells
so heavenly—
baking cinnamon rolls.
But the aunts say
they are for tomorrow's breakfast.
So Cooper and I grab
some store-bought cookies.
He and I go out to
the back porch.

TWO

"Did Colleen tell you
my secret?" I ask.
Cooper snorts.
"Colleen and I aren't
talking much these days."
"Kind of like Aunt Liz
and Uncle Dave today."
"Yeah."
"I heard my mom say
they're having problems."

"That's a shame.
I like Aunt Liz and Uncle Dave."
"Me too."

THREE
"So you don't know
my secret?"
"No."
"Well, it's not really
a secret.
My parents know.
I'm in love.
Sort of.
I think."

"But you're only eleven."
"I wish people would stop
saying that."
"Sorry."

"I didn't say
I was getting married.
I just like this boy
named Jimmy."

"You said 'love.' "
"But I said 'sort of.' "
"Okay."

"Do you have a girlfriend?"
"No."
"Did you ever?"
"Not really. I mean
I've liked some girls
better than others,
but I didn't
buy them flowers
or anything."

I show Cooper
my spider necklace.
"Jimmy gave me this."

"Don't let my mom see it,"
says Cooper.
"She even freaked out
when I brought home
a spider cookie
in my trick-or-treat bag!"

I yawn. "I guess I'll
go to bed now."
"Me too," says Cooper.
"I've been needing another kid
to talk to," I tell him.
"Me too."
"You're a nice cousin, Cooper."
"Thanks, Sophie."
"Buonanotte."
"Huh?"
"Good night, Cooper."

MIDNIGHT

Baby James is asleep—
finally!
Everyone
has gone to bed.
I've said good night
to Orange.
Tammy has stopped talking.
The rain patters

on the roof,
on the cars
in the driveway.
It sounds like
tiny silver
charms.

GHOST?

Suddenly
there is
a scream.
It's coming
from down the hall.
Has someone seen
a ghost?

It can't be.
There's no such thing
as ghosts . . .
right?

Not a Ghost

"It's a spider,"
says Aunt Nancy.
"A big, hairy spider—
right in the middle
of the bath mat.
I almost
stepped on it
in my bare feet!"

"Spiders eat the bad bugs,"
I whisper.

12:10 A.M.

Everyone
is up now
except for Baby James
and Colleen
and Orange.

We are sitting
in the kitchen.
Uncle Joe has his arm
around Aunt Nancy.
"It's okay, honey.
The spider is gone."

"Gone where?" says Mom.

"Maybe spider heaven,"
says Tammy.
"Maybe down the toilet,"
says Cooper.

"I'll make a nice pot
of mint tea,"
says Grandmom.
"Mint tea cures
almost anything."

Cooper nudges me,
whispers:
"I don't think
mint tea cures
arachnophobia."

JUST THE TOE

"Just your big toe,"
I say.
"I can't,"
says Cooper.
"I'll do it first, then,"
I tell him.
"My big toe.
Then your big toe.
Just in the surf.
Just for one second."

"I can't,"
says Cooper.
"Pleeease,"
I beg.
"I can't."
"Why not?"
"You know why not."
"Because you're scared."
"Don't say it so loud."
"I'm scared of the dentist."
"So?"
"So, I still go."
"But you can't drown
in a dentist chair."
"You can't drown
in a toe's worth of water, either."
"True."

TEST #1

Cooper: "Just my big toe, right?"
Me: "Right."
Cooper: "Just for one second."
Me: "One second."
Cooper: "O . . . kay."

Me: "Really?"
Cooper: "Yeah."

He does it:
one big toe in the ocean.
I'm so proud of my cousin,
I feel like throwing
my arms around him.
But I'm not sure how
he would feel about that.

Instead I shout:
"Way to go, Coop!"
He beams.

"Wait'll you see what comes next."
Cooper's eyes go wide.
"There's
a next?"

Just the Two of Us

In the afternoon,
Mom takes me aside.
"Let's slip away
for a little while.
Just the two of us."
We follow the path
behind the summerhouse
to a quieter beach.
We sit on
an old driftwood log,
facing the wide sky
and the ocean,
all shimmery and blue.

"Everything okay?"
Mom asks.
"Yep," I say. "Sort of."
Mom smiles.
"Tell me about
the 'sort of' part."

"Colleen is mad
at the world," I say.
"And that includes me."
"I think Colleen's
just having growing pains,"
Mom says.

"Growing pains?"
"It's a teenage thing."
"Does it hurt?"
"Not like a toothache."
"Like what, then?"
"Like being in a bad mood
you can't shake."
"Will I get growing pains?"
"Probably."

"Did *you* have
growing pains?"
"Oh yeah."

I giggle,
thinking of Mom
moping around
like Colleen.

"That's hard to believe,"
I say.
"Ask Grandmom."

"What cured you?"
Mom shrugs.

"Time . . .
and Grandmom's mint tea."

"Wow!" I say.
"So Grandmom's mint tea
actually works?"
Mom laughs.
"Not really.
I just got so tired
of drinking it,
I started acting cheerier
so she wouldn't keep making more."

"You were kind of pretending?"
"Kind of. And
a funny thing happened."
"What?"
"The pretending . . . ?"
"Yeah?"
"It became the real thing."
"You got nice again?"
She gives a thumbs-up.
"My old nice, wonderful self . . .
eventually."

Freedom

Finally
Orange the cat
is allowed
to roam the house.
She explores
every corner.
She sniffs
every cranny.
She rubs
up against
the table legs.
Then she hops
onto the green plaid chair
puddled with sunlight
next to the window
and purrs, purrs, purrs.

Another Letter

Dear Jimmy,
This is
my second letter.
I haven't gotten
a first letter

from you
yet.
I hope you
aren't sick.
I'm trying to help my cousin Cooper
to not be afraid
of the ocean.
I'm teaching my cousin Tammy Italian—
one word a day.
Today she asked me
to teach her the word for
"poopyhead"
because she's mad at Colleen, too.

Even if I wanted to
(which I don't),
I couldn't.
The word for "head"
is testa.
But the word for "poopy"
isn't in my book.

Write soon?

Your amica,
Sophie

An Outing with Grandpop

Every year at Summerhouse Time
Grandpop takes us grandkids
out for ice cream—
one at a time.
Today it's my turn.
Grandpop orders plain vanilla.
I get a hot fudge sundae—
wet nuts, whipped cream, extra cherries.

We sit outside
at a little round table
with a striped umbrella.
I point to Grandpop's ice cream.
"*Gelato*," I say.
He grins.
"I'm glad
you're studying Italian, Sophie.
Some of my favorite operas
are sung in Italian."

"I know," I tell him.
"You sing that song about
the moon

and pizza pie a lot.

It has the word *amore* in it.
Means 'love,' right?"

"Well, that song
isn't from an opera.
But it's fun to sing."

"Guess what, Grandpop."
"What?"
"I'm in *amore*."
"So I heard."

"There's a problem, though."
"What's that?"
"I sent him two letters—
and he hasn't sent me one."

Grandpop takes my hand.
"Maybe he's savoring your words.
And besides,
you can't hurry love.
That's another song."

UNCLE JOE'S JOB

Uncle Joe
isn't cooking tonight.
He had to
drive back to the city
to interview a guy
who makes fishing flies.
Uncle Joe is an editor
for a magazine called
Weekend Angler.
He can do most of his work
from home,

and even from the summerhouse,
on his computer.
Aunt Nancy
keeps his files in order,
makes his appointments,
takes his phone messages.
She likes to tell everyone
she's Uncle Joe's
unpaid personal assistant.

Uncle Joe says:
"I pay you in kisses
and smooshed spiders."

Aunt Nancy shivers
at the mention of spiders,
rolls her eyes,
and smiles.

TEST #2

"Just up to your ankles."
Cooper shakes his head.
"No way."

I tell him,
"I'll go first.
My ankles, then your ankles.
Just for a second."
"Nope."
"Nothing awful happened
with the toe test,
remember?"
"I remember, but . . .
I'm afraid."

I take a big chance.
I hook my little finger
into his little finger.
I'm afraid he'll pull away.
But he doesn't.
I stare into his eyes.
"Savor my words," I say.
"Huh?"
"You can do it.
Repeat after me:
I can do this."
"I can . . . do this."
"Again."
"I can do this."
"Okay, now do it."

And . . .
he does it!

THE BRIBE

Aunt Liz is chasing after Tammy.
"You need a bath."
"No!" says Tammy,
hiding behind a kitchen chair.
"That swimsuit
needs to be washed."
"No!" says Tammy,
scooting under the table.
Uncle Dave pipes up:
"You've been wearing
that monstrosity
four days straight."
"Yeah," says Cooper.
"It's starting to stink
like a rotten jellyfish."
"*You* stink like stinky socks,"
shouts Tammy.

"If you take a bath," I say,
"I'll let you borrow
my purple hair clip."

"I don't want it."

Uncle Dave rubs his head.
"What *do* you want?"

Tammy doesn't answer.
Uncle Dave kneels,
starts to crawl
under the table,
reaches up for Tammy.

Tammy screams:
"A hermit crab!
I want a hermit crab!"

Tammy,
clean, sweet-smelling
Tammy,
names her hermit crab
Samantha.
She holds Fuzzy Alligator
up to Samantha's cage.
"Samantha," she says,
"this is your brother,
Fuzzy Alligator."
Next she lifts Orange
up to the cage.
"And this is your cousin,
Orange the cat."
Orange wriggles
out of Tammy's arms.
Tammy waggles her finger
at Fuzzy and Orange.
"Now, you be
very nice
to Samantha!"

PHONE CALL

Aunt Liz gets a call
on her cell phone.
It's noisy here in the kitchen,
so she goes into
the living room.
She's in there a long time.
Uncle Dave says:
"I wonder
who she's talking to."

When Aunt Liz
doesn't come back
to the kitchen,
Uncle Dave goes into
the living room.
After a while
I see them both come out,
holding hands.
But Aunt Liz's eyes
are red-rimmed.
She sniffles,
blows her nose,
shakes her head.

I'm about to ask
when Cooper blurts out:
"Did somebody die?"

Letter #3

Dear Jimmy,
My aunt Liz lost her job.
Donations were down at the zoo.
Three people had to go.
Aunt Liz was one of them.
This means
no more free tickets,
no more Primate Pete.
By the way,
this is
my third letter to you.
(Not that I'm counting.)

Ciao!

Your amica,
Sophia

Insomnia

It's after midnight.
But unlike Tammy,
who is snoring
like a little outboard motor,
I can't sleep.

The grown-ups
are on the porch talking.
I can hear their voices
drifting up to my room
on the cool sea breeze.
But I can't quite hear
their exact words.

I've always liked
lying in bed
just like this,
listening to
the grown-ups'
nighttime chatter.
Except tonight I know
they are talking
about poor Aunt Liz's job.

Mom and I
are in the laundry room
folding towels.
I ask:
"Where are Uncle Dave and Aunt Liz?"
Mom says:
"In Biglerville, to pick up some things
from Aunt Liz's office."
"But they're coming back
to the summerhouse,
right?"
Mom hands me
another beach towel from the dryer.
"They'd better!
They left
Tammy and Baby James here."

I fold Tammy's mermaid towel.
"Things seem different here
this year."
Mom looks at me.
"How so?"
"Well . . . Colleen's mean and sad,

and Aunt Liz is worried and sad,
and it's not supposed to be like this
during Summerhouse Time.
Oh . . . and Jimmy Gabbiano
hasn't written to me once."
Mom tucks a strand of hair
behind my ear.
"Aren't you having a good time, honey?"
"I guess I am. It's just that last year
I was laughing all the time."
"And this year?"
"Not so much."

All of a sudden
Mom gets this
lopsided grin
on her face.
She stretches her arms
straight out,
flutters her fingers,
puts on her Dracula voice.
"I know just vat you need,"
she says.
(I think I know what's coming.)
"No!" I shriek.

"Vat you need is"—
Mom pounces—
"a *good tickle!*"
"Stop! Mom! Stop!"
But it turns out . . .
she's right!

ORPHAN

When I bring Tammy's towel
up to our room,
she's sitting on the bed.
Fuzzy Alligator is on her lap.
Tears are rolling down her cheeks.
"What's wrong?" I ask her.
"I'm an orphan!" she sobs.
I drape an arm around her.
"Who told you that?"
Tammy jabs her thumb
at Fuzzy Alligator.
"Him."
"Well, Fuzzy Alligator
is wrong.

Your parents
are coming back tomorrow."
"But Mommy doesn't have
a job anymore!" cries Tammy.
"I'm gonna be poor!"

I take my purse from my bureau.
Open it up.
I pull out six five-dollar bills.
I toss them in the air.
I tell her:
"Not as long as I'm around,
Tammy-ammy."

Dad is in the kitchen,
unloading a bag of vegetables
from Seaside Produce.
"Look at these tomatoes!"
He beams.
"Gorgeous!" says Mom.
"Tomatoes taste yucky,"
says Tammy.
"People used to think
they were poison,"
says Cooper.

Dad says: "Who can guess
the name of the person
who was the first to grow
a tomato in America?"
*Uh-oh, here comes
the history lesson.*
"Willy Wonka!" giggles Tammy.
"William Penn," says Cooper.
"Martha Washington," I say.
Dad waves the tomato at us:
"Thomas Jefferson!"

Next Dad holds up a cucumber.
"Okay, gang. Which president
ate cucumbers and vinegar
for breakfast?"
"Ewwwww!" says Tammy.
"Bill Clinton," says Cooper.
"Abe Lincoln," I guess.
"It was Ulysses S. Grant.
And just for the record,
President Lincoln hated being called Abe."

A carrot
is dangled in front of Mom's nose.
"Did you know that carrots were first grown
as medicine, not food?" Dad asks.

The counter is piled with vegetables.
I say to Tammy:
"Time for your word of the day."
"Okay, Soapy."
"Your word is:
la carota."
"What's that?" asks Tammy.
I dangle a carrot in front of her nose.
"It was once
a type of medicine."

I hardly ever see Colleen.
When I'm on the beach,
she's on the boardwalk.
When I'm in the kitchen,
she's on the porch.
When I'm working on my Italian,
she's watching TV.

Cooper is staying
clear of her.
But Baby James?
He seems to have
taken a liking
to grumpy Colleen.

He toddles after her,
dragging his teddy bear.
He tickles her toes
and giggles.
He reaches out to her.
His fat little arms say:
"Pick me up!"

At first
Colleen ignored him.
Now they seem to be
best buddies.

Sandy Road Chapel

"I found
the cutest church,"
says Grandmom.
"It's brand-new.
Just a few blocks away.
White with a blue door. Window boxes.
Pink geraniums.
I met Pastor Linda.
She's invited us all
to an ice cream social tomorrow afternoon."

"Ice cream! Ice cream!"
squeals Tammy,
as though she hadn't
just had two scoops
ten minutes ago.

Dad reminds us
that in 1784, George Washington
bought himself
his very own
ice cream machine.

Angels and Churches

Grandpop says
he's not one
for churches.

Grandmom says
they used to fight
about that
when they were younger.

Now
Grandmom
goes to church
by herself.

Grandpop
stays home
and reads the Sunday paper,
and they don't try
to change each other.

"What's to change?"
says Grandmom,
kissing Grandpop on the cheek.
"He's a keeper."

"What's to change?"
says Grandpop.
"I'm married to an angel.
That's church enough."

SCARY STORY NIGHT

"Welcome, bats and ghouls,
to Scary Story Night,"
says Uncle Dave
in the beachy firelight dark.

"I've got the marshmallows
and sticks," says Uncle Joe.

Dad has the driftwood fire going.
Sparks spatter like
tiny orange stars.
The air is cool.
We wrap ourselves in sweaters
and summer blankets.

"Me first!" cries Tammy.

Cooper wiggles his eyebrows.
"Oooooh, I'm already shaking."

TAMMY'S STORY

"Once upon a time,
there was a big hairy spider-monster."

"Eeek!" cries Aunt Nancy.
"Not a spider!"

"How big?" asks Cooper.

Tammy thinks for a minute.
"Big as a zebra!"

"Holy cow!" says Grandpop.

"Hush, everyone," says Grandmom.
"Let Tammy tell her story."

Tammy continues:
"The big hairy spider-monster was mean
and hungry.
He saw Uncle Joe
cooking spaghetti."

I tease Uncle Joe:
"You're in big trouble!"

Tammy shushes me.
"But the big hairy spider-monster didn't like
spaghetti."

"Whew!" says Uncle Joe.

"He liked people."

Cooper snorts.
"I thought you said it was a *mean* spider."

"The spider-monster liked to *eat* people.
He took a look at Cooper and said,
'That's my supper!' "

I pretend to take a bite out of Cooper's arm.
Cooper laughs.

"Then the spider saw Colleen.
He said to himself:
'That big girl looks dee-licious!'
Crunch-crunch!"

Colleen just pulls her sweater
up over the bottom part of her face.

"Then the big hairy spider-monster
saw Baby James."

At the mention of his name,
Baby James bounces on Colleen's lap
and grins and claps.

"And the big hairy spider-monster
said:
'Yum-yum!
There's my dessert.'

That's when Fuzzy Alligator turned into
Superhero Alligator.
He grabbed a fork and poked Hairy Spider
in his big hairy nose.

'You get out of our summerhouse right now,
big hairy spider-monster,'
said Superhero Alligator,
'or I will eat *you*!'

So Big Hairy Spider ran to the beach,
dove into the ocean,
and swam to California!"

Mom hugs Tammy.
"Fuzzy Alligator saved the day!"

"Yes, he did," says Tammy, all proud.
"The end."

More

Next, it's Uncle Dave's turn.
As usual, his story
features creatures
from outer space:
". . . and the slimy green slug from Mars
oozed through the pipes and up into the drain
of the summerhouse bathtub.
So when you take a bath,
watch out for . . ."

Colleen says she doesn't know any scary stories.

Mom has one:
"Once there was a ghost
who left rose petals on doorsteps,
and forever after those houses
were overwhelmed by
the sickly sweet odor
of dead roses."

Cooper tells about
an angry, crazy dentist:
"He kidnapped his patients
and pulled out all their teeth—
with no novocaine!"

I bop Cooper with my pillow.

And now
we're scary-storied out.
The night beach is still;
Baby James has fallen asleep
in Colleen's arms.
She drapes her sweater over him.

And
in the dying ember-glow,
I think I see
a tear
rolling down
Colleen's cheek.

A Message

When we get back
to the house,
there's a message
on Aunt Liz's cell phone.
It's from the director of the Biglerville Zoo.
Aunt Liz is so excited!
We crowd around her tiny phone
and listen:
"I got you
an interview with the folks at
Chanticleer Garden.
Next Wednesday. Ten a.m.

128 I told them what a wonderful job
you did for us.
They sounded
very interested."

Even Colleen
joins in the cheers!

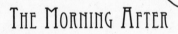

The Morning After

Most everyone sleeps late
the morning after
Scary Story Night.
Only Aunt Liz and I
are up.

"Want to go for donuts?"
she says.
We take two of the rented bikes
and head for the boardwalk
and Wally's Donuts.
The stand is run by the hippie man
who always wears
a tie-dyed T-shirt

under his apron.
There's a sign
tacked to the boards
that says:
MAKE DONUTS, NOT WAR!

"Two dozen assorted, please,"
says Aunt Liz.
"Plus one cinnamon twist."
(For Grandmom,
who doesn't care for donuts.)

Aunt Liz and I put the bags
in our wire bike baskets.
We start back.

Aunt Liz's hair is blowing.
She calls to the wind and me:
"Oh, Sophie, isn't it a glorious day!"

We soar past the shops.
We glide by
the sand and salt grass,
all sunlit and swishy.
Seagulls are screaming.

I swear they are saying,
"Look, they've got donuts!"

For a few seconds, I ride—
no hands,
arms out like wings.
For a few seconds,
I am a *gabbiano*,
flying, flying, flying.

Ice Cream Social

Grandpop may not be
one for churches,
but he is one
for ice cream socials,
even if they are
on church property.

He's even first in line.

Pastor Linda
dishes out scoops of
chocolate and vanilla.

There's a help-yourself table filled with
toppings:
butterscotch sauce,
chopped peanuts,
velvety chocolate sauce,
M&M'S,
fresh strawberries.

Soon the parking lot
is full of families

and couples
and sticky smiles.

I see Tammy
showing off Samantha to another little girl.

I see Cooper
ladling M&M'S, heaps of them,
into his paper bowl.

I don't see
Colleen
anywhere.

SOMETHING BAD

The inside of Sandy Road Chapel
is dim
and cool.
It smells of flowers and fresh paint.

The voices outside
are muffled
as if the ice cream social is underwater.

Colleen is sitting
in the back pew.
Her face is pale.
Her eyes are red.

I slip in beside her.
"Hi," I say.
She looks at me.
"Hi."
I take a deep breath.
I go for it:
"What's the matter?"

She looks away at the stained-glass windows.
Then she looks at me.
Her face is scrunched up.
She says something;
it comes out croaky and garbled,
but I recognize it—
it's my name:
"Sophie . . ."
Now I want to cry, too.
But then she says:
"I did something
very bad."

Imagining

What could this "bad"
be?
I start imagining stuff:
Colleen let a boy
do something to her?
Colleen flunked eighth grade
and didn't tell anyone?
Robbed a bank?
Smoked a cigarette?
Drank a beer?
What could it be?
And
do I really
want
to know?

Hush!

Tammy comes clomping in.
"Samantha wants to say a prayer."

She eyeballs Colleen.
"Why is Colleen crying?"

"Colleen isn't crying,"
I whisper-hiss.
"She just got sand in her eye.
And be quiet.
This is a church for people,
not crabs."

CROWD

We head back to the summerhouse
together,
the whole family,
like a school of fish.
There's zero chance
to be alone
with Colleen.

BRAVE

At the beach,
I'm ready to explode
from curiosity.
I've got to get Colleen alone.

I visit her blanket—
she's pretend-reading a paperback.
"Let's take a walk on the jetty,"
I say.
"Okay," she says.
But as soon as
she closes her book,
Cooper comes up, all excited.
"Knees!" he says.

"Knees?"

"Yeah—I'm *ready*."

"Right now?"

"I'm feeling *really* brave."

I look at Colleen.
"Cooper's feeling really brave,"
I say.

Colleen opens her book and turns away.
"Good for Cooper."

I slump.

Cooper says:
"Let's go!"

CARMEN

Most of the family
is going to the boardwalk.
Grandpop decides to stay
at the summerhouse.
The opera *Carmen*—
his favorite—
is on TV.

Colleen and I
decide to stay home.

Grandpop tells us
about *Carmen*.
"It's a love story,

sung in French,
about a Gypsy, a soldier,
and a bullfighter.
You two want to watch?"

Colleen winces.
Grandpop grins.
"Maybe another time."

We each give Grandpop a hug.
As we go to Colleen's room,
Grandpop's singing follows us:
"Le fleur que tu
m'avais
jetée!"
(I don't know any French.)

Finally

Colleen and I
are
alone.
Finally.

I feel
so
nervous.

What's she
going to
say?

The Confession

Colleen blurts it out:
"I stole three bags
of red licorice
from the supermarket."

I almost fall off the bed.
"But you *hate* red licorice!"
I squeal.

"It was the nearest stuff
to the store's door.
I stole it
just
for
fun."

"Was it fun?"

"Well,
it was
supposed
to be fun."

"Who told you that?"

"My new friend.
Sharon Ledbetter."

"Some friend," I say.
"Does your mom or dad know?"

"Nobody knows," says Colleen.
"Just you."

"And Sharon Ledbetter,"
I remind her.

"Right."

"Can you give the licorice back?"

"It's gone.
Mom found it where I stashed it,
in the back of the pantry.
She put it with the stuff
for the food bank.
She never knew it was stolen."

I borrow a phrase from Grandpop:
"Holy cow!"

"I feel awful."
"You've been acting awful."

"I know. One minute
I'm mad at myself.
The next
I'm mad at everyone else."

"It shows."

"Is everybody talking about me?"

"Mom and me.
We did."

"What did your mom say?"
"She said that you have growing pains."

Colleen gives a squeaky,
whispery sigh.
"I wish
that's all it was."

A Promise

I promise Colleen
I won't tell a soul.
I promise
I'll think about
what she should do.

Back in my room,
Tammy is squeaking
in her sleep.

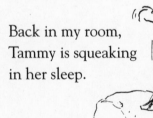

Orange is curled up
against my pillow.
I get my flashlight
and my notebook.
I turn to the first
blank page
and start making lists
for Colleen.

First List

Things You Might Possibly Do
1. Tell your mom and dad.
2. Tell Grandmom.
3. Tell Pastor Linda.
4. Let me tell my parents so they can tell yours.
5. Don't tell anyone.
Just buy three bags of red licorice
and sneak them back to the original store.
6. Mail the money for the licorice
with an anonymous note of apology
to the store manager.

Second List

Things You Positively Must Do
1. Never steal again.
2. Stop being friends with Sharon Ledbetter.
3. Start being nice to your favorite cousin (me).

The Plan

Colleen studies my lists.
She says:
"Sophie, for a kid
you're pretty smart."

I beam.

Colleen decides to do
the sixth item
on the first list.

"It's the easiest one,"
she says.

Dear Mr. Manager,
A month ago
I stole three bags
of red licorice
from your store.
I am as sorry as I can be.
I have promised my favorite cousin
that I will never
steal again.
Here is ten dollars
to cover the cost
of the candy.

Yours truly,
Anonymous

Secrets

Mom has told me,
lots of times—
there are two kinds of secrets.
There are secrets
we are not meant to keep—

like if somebody touches me
in a bad way.
Or somebody threatens
to do something harmful.
Then there are secrets
you must keep—
like if a friend tells me
her parents might be getting
a divorce
or that her coat
came from a yard sale.

And now
I'm feeling confused.

What kind of secret
is Colleen's?

ON THE SUMMERHOUSE PORCH

"I told Grandmom,"
Colleen whispers to me.
"About the licorice?"
I whisper back.

"Uh-huh. And about the letter
and the money.
And that you know
all about it."
"Oh my gosh!"
"Shhhh!"
(I forgot to whisper.)
"What did Grandmom say?"
"She said that she was proud of me
for telling.
And proud of you
for your good advice."
"Anything else?"
"Yeah. She said if I *ever*
do it again
she will personally ground me
for life
and make me drink mint tea
till it comes out
my ears."

Happy

Mom gets
a new swimsuit.

Aunt Liz gets
that job!

I get
a letter from Jimmy Gabbiano!

Life is good!

Mom's New Swimsuit

Mom's been wearing
Aunt Nancy's old swimsuit.
The one that split
in the back.
The one that Mom stitched.
And then it split again.
Dad had had it with that swimsuit.
He handed Aunt Nancy
a fistful of cash.
"Take my wife shopping.
Please!"

When Mom and Aunt Nancy return,
they are both beaming.
Mom holds up
a bright aqua swimsuit
with a starfish on the skirt.
"Fits perfectly," she says.
"And half price."

Aunt Nancy holds up
a pretty black and white swimsuit.
"I just couldn't resist it."

"Half price?" asks Uncle Joe.

Aunt Nancy laughs.
"You wish!"

Aunt Liz's New Job

Aunt Liz will start her new job
in September.

She will be
special-events coordinator
for Chanticleer Garden.
"Mommy," says Tammy,
"will there be
lions and tigers
in those gardens?"
Aunt Liz smiles.
"Well, kinda.
There'll be dandelions
and tiger lilies."
"Will they bite?"
says Tammy.

My Letter

Dear Sophie,
I got your letters.
I don't usually get mail
(except e-mail),
so it was fun.
I wrote an old-fashioned
pen-and-paper letter
to my grandmother once,

but this is the first one
I ever wrote to a friend.

So,
you will always be
the first friend
I ever wrote a letter to.
Ever.

Your really good friend,
Jimmy Seagull

DOCTORING SAMANTHA

"Samantha is sick,"
says Tammy.
"She's not eating
any of her lettuce."

"You put way too much lettuce
in her cage,"
says Cooper.

"She needs Grandmom's
mint tea,"
says Tammy.

Grandmom pulls
some of the lettuce leaves
out of Samantha's cage
and sets the kettle on to boil.

"This'll put her back
on her feet."

Grandpop says:
"I didn't know hermit crabs
had feet."

CATS ARE DIFFERENT

Samantha seems to
have gotten better.
(Was she ever
really sick?)

Tammy says:
"I'm taking Samantha

to the beach.
Why don't you
bring Orange?"

"Because
cats are different
from hermit crabs,"
I tell her.
"Samantha won't
run away.
But Orange might."

"But Orange
would come home,
right?"

"Maybe not.
Orange is just
getting used to
the summerhouse
again."

"Doesn't Orange
remember last year?"

"Not really.
Besides, the beach
is too busy.
It would be easy for Orange
to get lost."

"Hey, I got
a better idea—
you can take
Fuzzy Alligator
to the beach!"

"Okay, Tammy."

Restaurant Night

Every year,
we pick a really fun place
for a going-out dinner.

This year,
it's Cozy's Crab Shack
over by the bay.

Colleen did my hair
and gave me a manicure.
Tammy is wearing
a purple dress
over her mermaid swimsuit.
Baby James is wearing
a big, clean bib.

"It's such a lovely evening,"
says Aunt Nancy.
"Let's walk."
And so we do.
A caravan family
on many feet,
winding up one street
and down another.

Tammy races ahead.
"Wait at the corner, young lady,"
calls Aunt Liz.

Cooper gets all silly.
He grabs Grandmom
and dances her around
a Dumpster.

She laughs so hard,
she gets the hiccups.
Grandpop starts singing:
"O sole mio!"

People stare,
but the stares
are friendly
(I think).

They seem to be saying,
"What a nice family!"

And I think
we are.
Most of the time.

Cozy's Crab Shack

The hostess at Cozy's
leads us to their longest table,
way in the back
with a view of the bay
(if you are facing the window).

Tammy whines
that Cooper took her seat.
Baby James howls.
He doesn't want to sit
in the high chair.
He scoots away
from Uncle Dave—
smack into the knees
of our waitress.
Rolls and butter and bread plates
clatter to the floor.
She is very nice about it.
We help pick things up.
She does not wring
Baby James's little neck.

A man comes
with a dustpan and broom.

Tammy tells Baby James
the man is going to sweep *him* up.
More howling.
I hear Grandmom whisper to Grandpop:
"Better leave a *huge* tip."

Over in one corner,
a small band starts to play.
The music is so loud
I can't hear what Colleen
is saying to me
from across the table.

I turn to Dad,
who is next to me,
to ask if he'll change seats.

Dad's face is white.
He's breathing all funny.
His left arm is shaking.

Mom screams:
"Somebody call 911!"

DAD'S DIAGNOSIS

Dad was sure
he was having
a heart attack.
He says
he was never so scared
in his life.
He says
his heart was
beating really fast.
He says
he couldn't breathe.

In the emergency room,
they did a lot of tests.
When the doctor
finally returned,
Dad expected her to say:
You need surgery
immediately!
Instead the doctor said:
"Mr. Bolton, you've had
a panic attack."

"A panic attack?" I say.
"Is that better
than a heart attack?"

Dad smiles.
"Lots better."

Googling

The next day,
Colleen Googles
"panic attack."
She reads to me
from the screen:
"A panic attack
is a sudden unexpected period
of extreme anxiety.
It can mimic
a heart attack."

"What causes it?"

Colleen reads further:
"It can be caused by
caffeine or
some over-the-counter medications.

It can be caused by
severe stress
such as
loss of job
or divorce."

"Aunt Liz—
she lost her job!"
I exclaim.

"Nah," says Colleen.
"That doesn't count.
I think it has to be
the person himself.
What about
the divorce thing?"

"No way! Mom and Dad
would've told me,"
I say.

Colleen clicks off.

"I'll tell you one thing."
Colleen giggles.

"If we ever show our faces
at Cozy's Crab Shack again,
they're gonna lock the doors
and bar the windows
for sure!"

Relaxation Techniques

Relaxation techniques.
That's what the doctor
advised Dad to look into.

"First thing when we get home,"
says Mom, "we're going
right to the Book Bin.
They have an entire section
on stress."

"Deep breathing,
that's the ticket,"
says Uncle Joe.

"Have you ever tried
guided imagery?"
asks Aunt Liz.

"What's that?" says Cooper.

"It's when you lie down
and close your eyes—"

"Like a nap!" pipes up Tammy.

Uncle Dave shakes his finger at Tammy.
"It's Mommy's turn to talk."

Aunt Liz continues:
"You imagine yourself
in a favorite peaceful place. . . ."
"Like the summerhouse,"
says Colleen.

"But definitely *not like*
Cozy's Crab Shack," says Cooper.

"Music!" declares Grandpop.
"Music relaxes *me*."

Grandmom opens
her mouth to speak.
But before she can even say
one word,
we all shout:
"He needs
mint tea!"

Another Letter to Jimmy

Dear Jimmy,
My father had
a panic attack.
It might sound strange,
but I sort of feel good,
because I'd rather he had
a panic attack than a heart attack.
A panic attack comes from
too much stress.

*I am now trying to be
a no-stress daughter.
When you see me next,
I will be
the most easygoing person
you ever saw.*

Ciao!

*Your calm and cool amica,
Sophie*

P.S. *I loved your letter.*

Secret Mission

Uncle Dave is
all winks and grins.
He tells us
he is going on a mission.
We cousins *beg*
to go along.

"It's a *secret* mission.
I must go alone,"
he says, slipping out the door.

We cousins try to guess.
"He's going for fudge,"
says Cooper.
"No," says Tammy.
"He's going to buy me
those sparkly blue flip-flops
I wanted yesterday."

"I bet it's just more clams," says Colleen,
pinching her nose.
"What's so secret
about clams?" asks Cooper.

"Maybe," I say,
"he's *finally* replacing the frogs."

We all giggle.
Uncle Dave's swimsuit
has silly smiley frogs
all over it.

It was a gag gift
from a friend
for Uncle Dave's thirty-fifth birthday.
He was supposed to laugh.
He was supposed to toss it
in a drawer.
Instead
he's been wearing it
for *five years*.

WRONG

We are wrong
about the fudge,
the flip-flops,
the clams,
the frogs.

Uncle Dave is
all winks and grins
about kites!

Kites

There are kites for everyone.
Even Baby James.
Big kites.
Box kites.
Red kites.
Fish kites.
Dragon kites.
Even a mermaid kite.
Tammy grabs that one.
"Mine!"
Me,
I grab a dragon.

Waiting for a Windy Day

We listen
for wind chimes.

We watch
for flapping sails,
for salt grass
swaying,

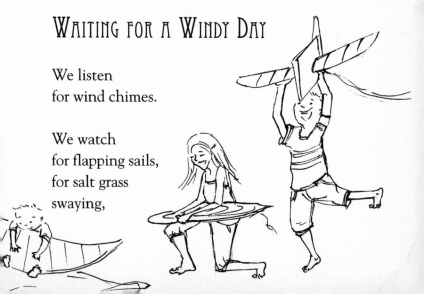

for blue waves
capping.

But all
is still.

Tammy drags
her kite
along the sand.

Day
after day
after day.

Ride Night

It's our night
for the rides:
roller coaster,
Ferris wheel,
Twisty Turtles
(for Baby James).

Mom says
maybe she and Dad
should skip the carnival.
All those lights,
so much noise,
screaming kids.

I don't want him to go.
What if Dad has
another panic attack?

"Not to worry," says Dad.
"They told me
just what to do."
He pats his pocket.
"They told me to
breathe into a paper bag."

Tammy hops up and down.
"C'mon, Aunt Jess!
C'mon, Uncle Mike!
We're missing
all the fun!"

Big Girl

Tammy tugs
at my father's sleeve.
"Take me on
the Sooper Dooper,
Uncle Mike.
Please! Please! Please!
I'm five this year.
I'm a big girl."

I remember
when I was five
and Dad took *me*
on the roller coaster.

I've been missing
stuff like that,
especially since Dad had
his panic attack.

It's like I want to
plop onto his lap,
tickle him
under his chin,

tell him,
"I love you
as high as the sky!"

But I'm a too-big girl now.
Right?

Roller Coasters

There are two
roller coasters
on the pier.
The Sooper Dooper
is tall, with glittering lights
looping far over the water.
You have to be forty-five inches tall
to ride on it.
Tammy is
forty inches tall
on her tiptoes.

So Dad takes her on
the Silver Dragon.
Not as tall.
Not as loopy.

Tammy waves at me.

Click,
click,
click,
up the track
slow-ly,
then . . .
WHOOSH!
Down like a comet,
with every inch of Tammy
screaming like a happy maniac.

Good thing
Dad has
his trusty paper bag.

The Ferris Wheel

ONE
I ask Colleen:
"Do you really
hate the Ferris wheel?"

"Nah. I just said that
because I was
mad, sad, and feeling bad."

"So—do you want to
go on
with me?"

"Let's go!"

TWO
"Mind if we join you?"
Grandpop and Grandmom
are going on
the Ferris wheel, too.
We see them
in the seat below us.

We hear Grandmom
scolding Grandpop.
"Stop rocking!"
But we also hear
a smile in her voice.
And we know she kind of likes
the rocking.

THREE
Colleen and I
are at the very top.
We're stopped.
Ship lights blink
across the dark sea.
The pier below
is a wild splash of neon.
People look tiny.
Music rises and becomes softer.
Store managers
and big mistakes
seem smaller
and as distant
as the pale moon.
Colleen looks over at me,
squeezes my hand,
smiles.

I feel . . .
melty.
I have
my cool Colleen back.

Bare Baby

Some of us are at
the local drugstore.
Aunt Liz needs toothpaste.
Tammy doesn't need anything.
She just wants to buy
something.
Dad needs nail clippers.
I'm looking for
a new cat toy for Orange.
Her catnip mouse is gone.
Tammy is blaming Fuzzy Alligator.

Aunt Liz calls for Baby James.
I head over to the toy aisle.
Yep—he's there—

naked as President John Quincy Adams
in the Potomac.

In one hand,
he is holding a rubber shark.
In the other, his swimsuit.
He shrieks when he sees me
and races down the aisle.

I hear an older lady
telling the cashier:
"Excuse me,
but there's a naked boy
in your store."

The cashier must have thought
the lady meant
a *big* naked boy—
she calls security!

Back at the summerhouse,
Tammy tells the others
how Baby James
went to jail.

Today
Tammy wants to put on
a magic show.

She grabs the laundry basket.
In goes
Uncle Joe's wooden spoon
(magic wand).

In goes
Aunt Nancy's black sweater
(magic cape).

In goes
the banana from the fruit bowl
(microphone).

In goes
Samantha and Fuzzy Alligator
(magician's assistants).

Next,
Tammy drags the basket
out to the deck
(stage).

She leaves the door open
and
out goes Orange.

It happens so fast—
Orange flashing past
onto the beach,
losing herself
in a crayon box of color:
blue umbrellas,
yellow beach balls,
purple towels,
red sand pails . . .
my orange cat.
Gone.

Cooper says:
"The magician made
the cat disappear."

My Reply

I say:
"That's
not
funny,
Cooper!"

Blame

Tammy sobs:
"It was Fuzzy Alligator's fault!
It was *his* job
to close the door!"

Search Party

Dad and the uncles
head for the beach
to search for Orange.

"I want to go, too,"
I say.

Dad says
it's best for me to stay
at the summerhouse.

Best for me to be here
in case Orange
finds her way back.

APOLOGIES

Cooper says:
"I'm sorry, Sophie.
I know it wasn't funny."

Tammy says:
"I'm sorry, too, Soapy.
I'm going to
ground Fuzzy Alligator
for the whole rest of the vacation."

"Now, Tammy," says Aunt Liz,
"it wasn't his job
to close that door.

That was *your* job.
You know better than that."

"You're the one
who should be grounded,"
says Cooper.

Colleen pokes her brother.
"Mind your own business."

Tammy sniffles:
"Yeah, Cooper-pooper."

"That's enough, Tammy,"
says Aunt Liz.

Colleen says:
"What do *you* say, Sophie?"

I say:
"I'm really,
really
upset."

Grandmom says:
"Time for mint tea!"

MAD

No stupid tea
can fix
the crack in my heart.

I go to my room,
curl up on the bed,
hug my pillow and
Orange's new fish toy.

Tammy taps at the door.
"Can I come in
and say I'm sorry, Soapy?"

"No."
(I'm so mad at her.)

Cooper knocks next.
"I'm going to
look for Orange, too, Sophie."
(I'm still mad at him.)

Colleen doesn't knock at all.
This makes me mad, too.
Where *is* she?

Downstairs drinking stupid mint tea?
Eating stupid cookies?

I'm too mad to eat.
I'm too mad to talk.
I'm too mad to write a letter.

But I scribble a fast postcard
to Jimmy Gabbiano.

Orange is lost.
Perduto.
I'm sad.

LITTLE KID

Mom calls through the door:
"Sophie, honey,
I'm coming in."

She sits on the bed.
She pulls me onto her lap.
I feel like a little baby,
back in my mom's arms.
Safe enough to
cry
   and cry
      and cry.

Maybe

It's dinnertime.
Dad and the uncles
are back.
They bring
take-out seafood for supper.
But they don't bring
Orange.

"We'll look again tomorrow,"
says Dad,
hugging me.
"Promise."

I give him my best
stress-free smile.

"Maybe Orange
will come home tonight,"
says Grandmom.

"It might be easier
for her to find us
when the beach is empty,"
says Aunt Nancy.

No Reply

Uncle Joe fills me a plate.
"Not hungry," I say.

"No dinner
for poopy Fuzzy Alligator!"
says Tammy.

"If Sophie's not eating,"
says Cooper,
"then neither am I."

"What about Colleen?"
asks Uncle Joe.
"Colleen loves shrimp."

Aunt Nancy calls up the stairs:
"Colleen—dinner!"

No reply.

Colleen
is not in her room.
Not on the deck.
Not anywhere in the house.
And it's starting
to get dark.

BRACELET

Dad and the uncles
are about to go search,
when in comes Colleen,
carrying a bag.

She empties it on the table:
poster board,
markers,
tape.

"We can all make posters:
LOST CAT.
ANSWERS TO THE NAME OF ORANGE.
REWARD!!"

"Reward?"
says Cooper.

"Twenty dollars,"
says Colleen.
"I sold my charm bracelet
to the jeweler on the boardwalk."

I gasp.
"Your favorite bracelet!"

Colleen puts her arms around me.
"Hey, I can always get
another dumb bracelet."

Keeping Watch

I am going to stay awake
all night on the deck.
I am going to be here
for Orange
when she comes back.

Great Idea

"Honey, you probably can't
stay awake all night," says Mom.

"I have an idea," says Cooper.
"We can take turns.
We can stay up in shifts.
The whole family."

"Except for Tammy
and Baby James," says Colleen.

"I can take a turn!"
cries Tammy.

"Count me in," says Grandpop.

"Great idea!" says Grandmom.

"I'll take
the midnight-to-one shift,"
says Aunt Liz.

Colleen prints out a schedule
on the last piece of poster board.
My shift is nine to ten p.m.,
starting now.

Come home, Orange.
Come home.
Come home.
Come home.

Cooper's Shift

Ten to eleven p.m.
is Cooper's shift.
He comes out to the deck
in his pajamas.

He pats my shoulder.
"No luck, huh?"

I sigh.
"Not yet."

Sad Sunny Day

This morning is
all sun,
blue sky,
seagulls swooping.
But only Baby James is smiling.

Last night
the whole family
watched,
waited,
hour by hour,
but Orange
didn't find her way
back to us.

Who said sunny days
are happy days?

Orange Lost: Day Two

After breakfast,
the uncles and aunts
go looking for Orange.

Colleen heads for the boardwalk
to tape up
the LOST CAT posters.

Dad decides to check
the local animal shelter
and the lost and found
near the pier.
"Can't hurt," he says.

Mom and Grandmom
have to stay home
to take care of
Tammy and Baby James.

I stand on the deck,
searching through
all the colors on the beach—
the blues and reds,
purples and yellows
and greens—

hoping for
a glimpse of Orange.

A Little Prayer

Grandpop
comes out to the deck.
He stands beside me.
"Maybe we should
say a little prayer."

I gape at him.
"But you *never*
go to church, Grandpop."

"But I do pray, Sophie.
Especially at times like this."
He takes my hand in his.
"Let's say a silent prayer
for Orange."

I don't know
what Grandpop said to God,
but here's what I said:

Dear God,
Please help Orange find her way back
to our summerhouse.
Please keep her safe
while she is looking for us
and we are looking for her.
Please forgive me
for getting mad at Cooper.
And for thinking
that Colleen didn't care.
And help me to stop being
so mad at Tammy.
In case you missed it—
she's the one who
left the door open.
Amen.

THE WIND KICKS UP

"It's windy!" shouts Tammy.
"Lookit the sails flapping!
Get the kites!"

"Not today," says Grandmom.

"How come? It's windy!"

"Because we're still sad
about Orange."

"Can't sad people fly kites?"

"They can," says Grandmom.
"But they usually
don't feel like it."

"Well,
I feel like it," says Tammy.
"But I'm still sad.
Promise."

Walking with Dad

That night,
Dad and I
go for a walk
along the beach.

"Do you think
Orange will come back?"
I ask.

"Truth?" says Dad.

"Truth."

"I'd be surprised, honey.
Orange has been gone
a long time for a cat."

"But we can still
watch for her?"

Dad squeezes my hand.
"Absolutely.

As a matter of fact,
I'm down tonight
for a double shift."

"Dad, that's too much.
You're doing enough."

Dad waves it off.
"Hey, waiting for Orange
to show up
is easy duty.
She's my family, too."

After My Shift

I hear Tammy sleep-squeaking.

I hear Samantha scratching
across her cage.

At ten-thirty, I hear
Grandmom taking her bath.

At eleven, I hear
Aunt Liz
brushing her teeth.

At midnight, I hear
Baby James howling.

After that I hear
Grandpop coughing
in the kitchen,
making toast,
trying to be quiet.

The hours pass.
The sun comes up.
If the sun made noise
I would hear that, too.

I hear everything
but the patter
of cat paws.

A Long Talk with Mom

PART ONE

Mom says:
"Only five more days
at the summerhouse."

A tear trickles down my cheek.
"We *can't* go home.
What if Orange
comes looking for us?"

Mom drapes her arm around me.
"We'll tell the next family
who rents the summerhouse
to keep an eye out
for Orange."

"Can we ask *them* to do shifts?"

But I know the answer to that
even before
Mom opens her mouth.

Mom says:
"No more shifts
for our family, either."

I screech:
"Why not?"

"Because it isn't working, Sophie.
And it isn't fair.
It isn't fair to Grandmom and Grandpop.
Sleep is important to them."

"Then I'll do their shifts."

"And it isn't fair
to ask your aunts and uncles
to spend all their time searching.
This is their vacation."

"But, Mom,"
I say,
"Orange isn't just a cat.
She's our family."

"So are your cousins.
And they don't want to do things
while you're feeling sad."

"Tammy still wants to do things,"
I snort.

"Tammy's a little girl, Sophie.
She didn't mean to
leave the door open.
You're being too hard on her."

PART THREE

"So, what are you saying, Mom—
I should forget about Orange?"

"Not at all, honey.
I'm saying you can't
expect everyone
to feel as sad as you do."

"So you want me
to tell Cooper and Colleen
they can start having fun again?"

"Worth thinking about."

"Tammy, too?"

"That would be nice."

PART FOUR
"Just as long as you know, Mom,
I'm not letting myself
off the hook.
I don't intend to have
any fun at all."

"You might want to rethink that,"
says Mom.

"What's to rethink?
This is our Summerhouse Time.
Our perfect time.
It's supposed to be just like always.
Only this year it's all wrecked."

Mom gives me a squeeze.
"Sophie, here's a news flash for you:

Life is never perfect,
even at the summerhouse."

Walking the Surf

Life is never perfect.
My mother's words fall on my ears
over and over like the ocean waves
as I walk barefoot in the surf.

I think of three summers ago,
when Colleen and Cooper
didn't speak to each other because
Cooper snuck behind Colleen
on the boardwalk
and shouted, "Boo!"
and made her drop
her chocolate-covered frozen banana.

I think of two summers ago,
when Aunt Nancy lay in the sun too long
and looked like a cooked lobster
and had to stay in the house
for four days.

I think of last year,
when we all ate something bad—
Grandpop thinks it was oysters—
and spent two days
running to the bathroom.
Yuck!

Not that any of those things
are like the catastrophe
of losing Orange,
but I guess Mom is right—
maybe even Summerhouse Time
hasn't been as perfect
as I remember.

We all laugh about those things now.
Maybe someday—please—we will laugh
about the Summer Orange Got Lost
and Came Back.
Please.

Gone

Later that day
I tell Tammy:
"It's okay
if you want to
fly your kite."

Tammy points
to the sails drooping.
She pouts.
"The wind is all gone."

"It'll come back,"
I tell her.
"It always does."

To the Church

Grandmom decides
to bring some of
Uncle Joe's
famous blueberry scones
over to Pastor Linda.

I go with Grandmom.
I pretend to be cheerful.
We talk about
the murder mystery
she is reading.

We get to the manse,
knock on the door.
Pastor Linda
isn't home.

We cross the parking lot
to the church.
Pastor Linda
is there,
near the altar,
and so is . . .
Orange!

MEMBER OF THE FAMILY

"Orange!" I scream,
racing
to the front of the church.

I lift my cat
and hold her high
and dance around.
I nuzzle her
up one side
and down the other.
She meows.
I cry the good tears.

"Orange?"
says Pastor Linda.

"The cat's name,"
explains Grandmom.
"Orange is a very
important member
of our family.
We've been
missing her."

Two Words

Uncle Dave calls it
"se-ren-dip-i-ty."
Serendipity means
when something wonderful
happens by accident.

Grandmom has
another word for it:
"miracle!"

I have two words:
"*Grazie*, God."

Here's What Happened

A nice lady found Orange
wandering on the beach.
She fed Orange
some of her
tuna fish sandwich,
and Orange followed
the nice lady

to her room at
the Sea Breeze Motel.
But not for long:
NO PETS ALLOWED.

So the nice lady
borrowed a picnic basket
and carried Orange
to Sandy Road Chapel.
She figured that Pastor Linda
would know what to do.

Pastor Linda
took Orange in.

And for a day or two,
Orange was
a church cat.

Reward

Colleen insists
that Pastor Linda
keep the reward money.

"Well," says Pastor Linda,
"the church could use
a card table
for coffee hour."

"With an orange tablecloth!"
pipes up Tammy.

An Orange Party

It's a party!
Uncle Joe makes a cake
with orange frosting.
Grandmom spells out
Welcome Home Orange
with chocolate chips.
Aunt Liz pours lemonade.
Aunt Nancy plays
a Bruce Springsteen CD.
Grandpop sings along.
Colleen dances with Baby James—
he loves it!

Tammy dances with Fuzzy Alligator
while Samantha and her cage
dangle from her wrist.
(Do hermit crabs
like music?)
Cooper plays Scrabble
with Dad and Uncle Dave.
I sit in the corner
with Orange curled on my lap,
soaking in the miracle
of Summerhouse Time.

WIND!

On our last summerhouse day
we wake up to wind chimes
and flapping sails,
salt grass swaying,
blue waves capping.
"Get the kites!"
I yell.

We all
race down to the beach,
sunlight on our faces,
kites rising skyward,
our laughter on the wind.
Baby James
bounces in his stroller,
howling,
screaming,
clapping his hands
for windy joy.

Very Last Night

Last night,
Tammy and I
slept in Colleen's bed—
that made three of us—
Tammy in the middle.
A cousin sandwich.
Then Cooper came in and
unrolled his sleeping bag
on the floor.

"Next year," he said,
"I'm going to ride the waves."
Colleen gave a giggle.
"Next year,
I'm getting
a bikini—lime green!"
Cooper snorted. "Ha!
Dad won't let you."
"Next year,
I'm going to make sure
Fuzzy Alligator
always shuts the door,"
said Tammy.
"Next year,
I'm going to ride
the *big* roller coaster,"
I told them.
"Next year,
we'll all be one year older,"
said Colleen.
"And one year bigger,"
said Tammy.
"I'll be able to ride
the Sooper Dooper
with Soapy."

Last night,
Dad tapped on the door.
"Aren't you kids
ever going to sleep?"

And we yelled:
"*NO!*"

Final Morning

This morning,
the cars are packed.
Orange is peeking out
from the back car window.
Grandmom shuts the door
to the summerhouse
and slips the key
under the mat.

Baby James howls.
"Be quiet!" scolds Tammy.
"You're scaring Samantha."

Cooper scuffs the sand
with the toe of his sneaker.

He says:
"Thanks for getting me
into the ocean, Sophie."

I tuck my prettiest shell
into Colleen's pocket.
"Don't forget
your favorite cousin."

Aunt Nancy plops down
on a deck chair.
"Why can't we stay
forever?"

Grandpop starts singing:
"Ar-ri-ve-der-ci Roma!"
Uncle Dave joins in.
People walking past them grin.

Mom calls for a group hug.
Uncle Joe hands out
bags of oatmeal cookies
for the road trips home.

I am kissed
and kissed and kissed.
Nobody wants to leave.

DON'T CRY

Our car heads out first.
I wave and wave.
I return Tammy's
blown kisses.
My eyes fill up.
I stroke Orange.
"Don't cry,"
I tell her.

In just a wink
it will be next year
and Mom will be calling out:
"C'mon, everybody—
it's Summerhouse Time!"

Half-Awake

Orange falls asleep
on my lap.
I'm too excited
for sleep.
I can't wait to see
my best friend, Katie,
and to introduce her to
Jimmy Gabbiano.

New school year.

I guess I'm ready.

If I have to write
a paper on what I did
this summer,
I'll be able to fill up
a whole notebook!

DATE DUE			